Looking for Yesterday

Happiness… not in another place but this place,
not for another hour but this hour.
— Walt Whitman

For Mark and Lucy—I hope all your todays
and tomorrows are the best. Love from Alison.

First U.S. edition 2019
First published by Old Barn Books (U.K.) 2017

Library of Congress Catalog Card Number pending
ISBN 978-1-5362-0421-6

19 20 21 22 23 24 TWP 10 9 8 7 6 5 4 3 2 1

Printed in Johor Bahru, Malaysia

This book was typeset in Bellota Regular.
The illustrations were created using alkyd oil paints.

Candlewick Press
99 Dover Street
Somerville, Massachusetts 02144

visit us at www.candlewick.com

Looking for Yesterday

Alison Jay

CANDLEWICK PRESS

Yesterday was the best day.

I wish I could go back and do it all again.

But how?

I know that when you look at the stars,
you are looking at light from a million yesterdays.

I would need to go faster than light — one hundred and eighty-six thousand miles per second . . . over seven and a half times counterclockwise around the earth every second . . . . to get back to yesterday.

What goes faster
than light?

A bus can't travel at superluminal speed.

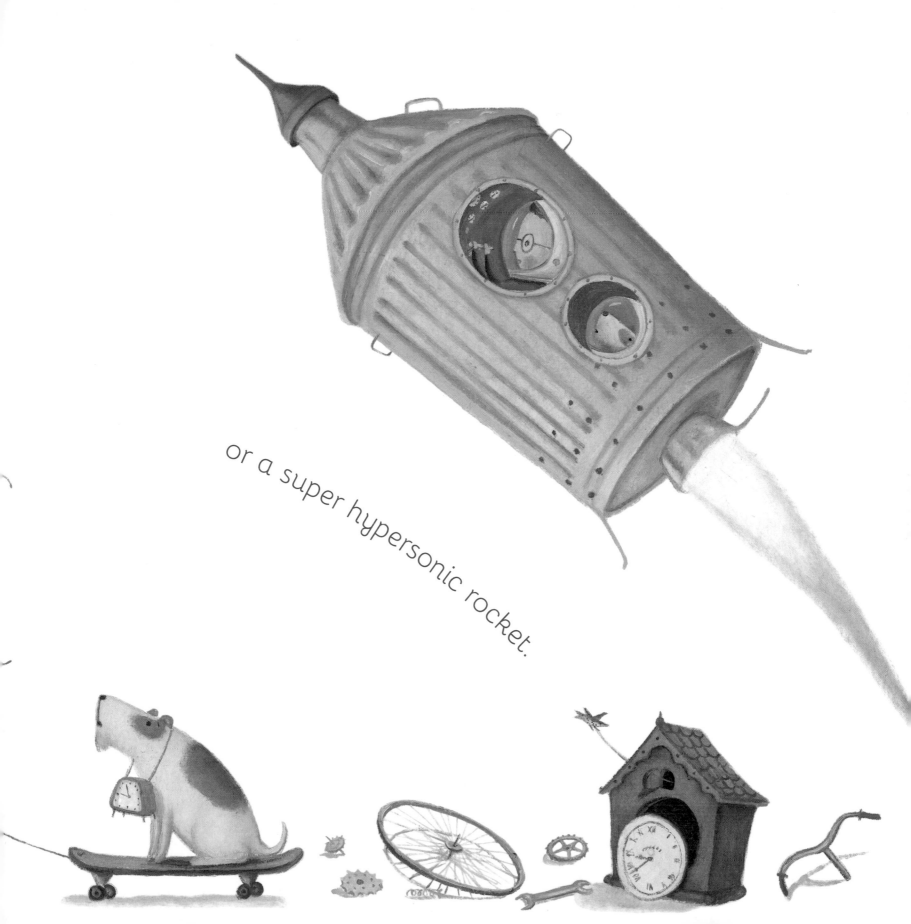

or a super hypersonic rocket.

Or, some scientists say there are wormholes in space that could take us back in time.

I've just got to find one!

(And shrink myself to one billion
trillion trillionths of a centimeter!)

Granddad, can you help me to find the way back to yesterday?

"Why do you want to go back to yesterday?"

"Because it was the best day, Granddad!"

"Yesterday was a wonderful day, but there are many more happy days to come.

Let me tell you about some of my best days.

"I have seen ten thousand birds fly through a sunset.
I have seen bright lights shimmer across a black sky.

I have danced by moonlight with the love of my life.

I have laughed until dawn with friends old and new.

"I have floated through clouds . . ."

and over thundering water.

"I have climbed high to the top of a snow-capped mountain...

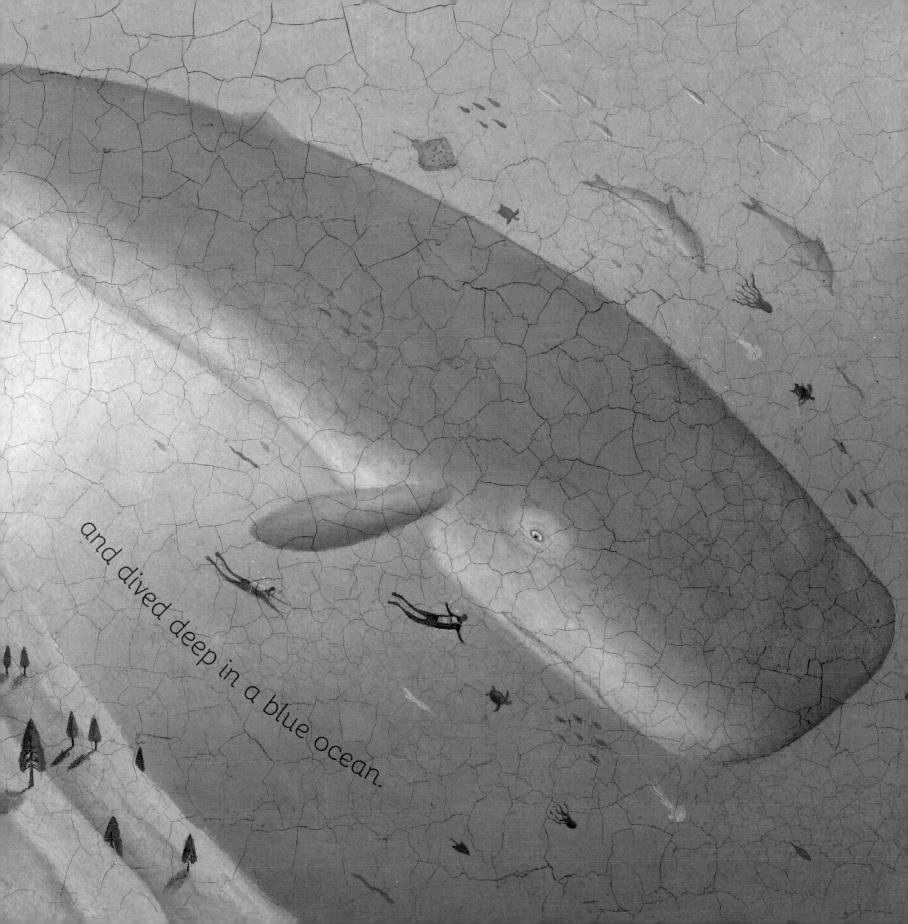

and dived deep in a blue ocean.

"Our best days make happy memories.

But every day brings the chance of a new adventure.
Why go looking for yesterday when you can be happy here...

"TODAY!"